VENUS AND SERENA
WILLIAMS

VENUS AND SERENA WILLIAMS

GABRIEL FLYNN

THE CHILD'S WORLD®, INC.

ON THE COVER...

Front cover: Venus (left) and Serena (right) smile after their match in the Australian Open Tennis Championships on January 21, 1998.
Page 2: Serena (left) and Venus (right) pose for a picture before their match against each other in the 1998 Australian Open.

Library of Congress Cataloging-in-Publication Data
Flynn, Gabriel.
Venus and Serena Williams / by Gabriel Flynn.
p.   cm.
Includes index.
Summary: Describes the childhood and accomplishments
of the teenaged professional tennis players who
share the goal of becoming the only sisters ranked
number one and two in the world.
ISBN 1-56766-664-7 (lib. reinforced. : alk. paper)
1. Williams, Venus, 1980– .
2. Williams, Serena, 1981– .
3. Tennis players—United States Biography Juvenile literature.
4. Afro-American women tennis players Biography Juvenile literature.
[1. Williams, Venus, 1980– . 2. Williams, Serena, 1981– .
3. Tennis players. 4. Women Biography. 5. Afro-Americans Biography.]   I. Title.
GV994.W49F59   1999
796.342'092'273—dc21   99-24146
[B]   CIP
                                AC

PHOTO CREDITS

All photos © AP/Wide World Photos

TABLE OF CONTENTS

SISTERS

It is the mid-1980s in the **ghetto** of Compton, California, just south of Los Angeles. Life is hard. Garbage and broken glass lie in the streets. Crime is high, and buildings are covered with spray-paint called **graffiti.** In the middle of this city are run-down tennis courts. The fences are rusty, the courts are cracked, and the nets need repair. Does anybody even use these courts?

"Whoosh" goes the ball as one family plays. This is the Williams family: a dad, a mom, and five daughters. The two youngest daughters are Venus and Serena. They show the most interest and play every chance they can.

HOW THEY GOT STARTED

How did the Williams family get interested in tennis? Richard says he was watching a tournament on TV and saw the champion get a check for a lot of money. He told his wife, Oracene, "Let's put our kids in tennis so they can become millionaires." And that's what they did.

 Serena (left) and Venus (right) playing during a doubles match in the Italian Open on May 7, 1998.

Throughout Venus's and Serena's childhood, their parents were their coaches. This was very unusual. Not only had their parents never coached, but they didn't even know how to play tennis! Many people said that someone else should have been their coach. But famous tennis coach Nick Bolletteiri disagrees. He says, "The road they've gone on couldn't have been better selected. ...Nobody knows those girls better than their parents."

Venus and Serena began playing in the United States Tennis Association (USTA) for kids. They were the best players in their area. By age 10, Venus had already won 30 titles and was **ranked** number one in the 10-12 age group.

Although Venus and Serena were very good, they didn't play in as many tournaments as most other girls. This was because their parents wanted them to focus on school.

CHANGING COACHES

When Venus was 11, the Williams family moved to Palm Beach Gardens, Florida. There they could play against better competition. Their house had a tennis court in the backyard. They also began training with professional tennis coach Richard Macci. He stated that Venus was so competitive that she would "run over broken glass to hit a ball." His practice schedule was very hard. They practiced six hours a day for six days a week. They also had to hit 200 serves every day.

Venus returns a shot to Ai Sugiyama of Japan during their match at the Evert Cup on March 9, 1997.

After 1½ years, Richard decided that he and Oracene should coach the girls again. Many people thought this was a bad decision, but not Macci. He said Richard "has done what he thought in his heart was best for his girls." Would they make it in professional tennis being coached by their parents? The world was waiting to see.

A BIG SPLASH ON THE PROFESSIONAL TOUR

Venus and Serena are different from many other tennis players. They are **African-American**, and there are very few African-American professional tennis players. The two are lively and shout and jump a lot on the court. They wear bright clothes and play with colorful beads in their hair. "Me and Serena are a whole different thing happening," said Venus. Venus is the taller, faster player. Her best shots are her serve and her overhead smash. Serena is shorter and has a more muscular body. She beats people with her powerful backhand. Both sisters are very strong.

Just how strong are they? At Wimbledon in 1998, Venus slammed a serve at 125 miles per hour. It was the fastest serve by a woman ever! Then, in the 1998 European Championships, she played Mary Pierce. "Wham!" She broke her own world record with a serve at 127 miles per hour! Venus said, "I've just turned 18 so I'm just going to get stronger.... In the last year, I gained 9 miles per hour on my serve." Serena's fastest serve was 112 miles per hour.

Venus slams a powerful serve against Martina Hingis during their match at the Evert Cup on March 13, 1998.

11

THE U.S. OPEN

In 1997, Venus played in the U.S. Open. This important tournament was played in brand-new Arthur Ashe Stadium in Flushing Meadow, New York. The stadium was named after Arthur Ashe, the most famous African-American tennis player of all time. Venus wanted to play in the U.S. Open to show that other African-Americans can be good at tennis. Venus said, "I think with this moment in the first year in Arthur Ashe Stadium, it all represents everyone being together, everyone having a chance to play."

She was **unseeded,** which means she was supposed to be one of the worst players in the tournament. But she played well and surprised the other players. She won all her matches and made it to the championship match.

In the championship, she played the world's number one-ranked player, Martina Hingis. Venus played hard but lost. Although she lost, she made history. She was the first unseeded player ever to reach the finals. She was also the first African-American woman to reach the finals since 1958!

The world began to see that Venus was going to be a top player. Hingis said, "For the first time she showed that she can play great." But could Venus and Serena truly become great? That is what they set out to prove.

Venus follows through on a serve from Larisa Neiland of Latvia at the U.S. Open on August 25, 1997.

MOVING UP

In 1997, Serena was ranked number 453 in the world. Only eight months later, she rose to number 20. With her powerful backhand she played well in seven tournaments. One of those was in Sydney, Australia. There she beat the world's number two-ranked player, Lindsay Davenport.

Although she earned her high ranking by using her talents, Serena gave the credit to the coaching of her dad. She said, "If it wasn't for my dad, I definitely wouldn't be here today. He always keeps my confidence up."

Venus also moved up in the rankings. Her father taught her to keep using her strong serve and overhead smash. She said, "All my career I've had people ask when I was going to get a real coach…. Now, hopefully, people see that our parents knew what they were doing."

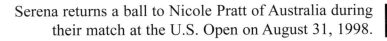

Serena returns a ball to Nicole Pratt of Australia during their match at the U.S. Open on August 31, 1998.

THE LIPTON CHAMPIONSHIPS

In 1998, both Venus and Serena played in the Lipton Championships in Oklahoma City, Oklahoma. Serena was unseeded, but she amazed the tennis world by beating three players in a row. She then had to play Martina Hingis, the top-ranked player in the world. It was a tough match, and Serena lost in a tiebreaker. Although she was knocked out of the tournament, she was finally recognized as one of the best new players. Her world ranking soared. But what about Venus?

Venus was also playing well. She won her first four matches without losing a **set,** which is a group of games in a tennis match. Now it was her turn to play Hingis. It took three sets, but Venus won. She beat the best player in the world!

She was now was in the championship match against Anna Kournikova. It was a tough match that also took three sets. Venus lost the first set, but she began to play better and won the second set. Serena and her mother cheered her on. The final set took only 26 minutes. With her powerful serve, Venus won that set, too!

Venus was now ranked number 10. Only one other player has ever moved up so quickly in the computer rankings. But when Venus accepted her trophy, she wasn't thinking of her ranking. She was thinking of her family. She said, "When I win, everyone wins— Serena wins, my mom wins.… It helps Serena … because when I win, I can tell her what I did to win."

Venus smiles as she holds the Lipton Championship trophy after beating Anna Kournikova on March 28, 1998.

GRAND SLAM SWEEP

Yes, 1998 was a good year for the Williams sisters. They even did better playing **mixed doubles.** In mixed doubles, a man and a woman play together against another man and woman. In tennis, the four biggest tournaments are called the Grand Slam. These tournaments are the U.S. Open, the Australian Open, the French Open, and Wimbledon. Venus's mixed doubles partner was Justin Gimelstob. They won the Australian and French Opens. Serena's mixed doubles partner was Max Mirnyi. They won the U.S. Open and Wimbledon. It was a Grand Slam **sweep** for the Williams sisters!

HEADING FOR THE FUTURE

Venus and Serena keep climbing in the world rankings. Going into 1999, Venus was ranked number three in the world. Serena was ranked number eight. Will they be able to keep on winning and be ranked number one and number two in the world? Venus said, "I'm not going to just be playing tournaments for the sake of it, I'm going to be there to compete hard." Serena said, "I feel I'm getting stronger all the time.... I really think this is going to be my year and that I can break through into the top level." Who does Serena thank for helping her to reach her dream? She said, "I thank my sister. She's been an inspiration."

Serena smiles as she holds the trophy she and Max Mirnyi won for mixed doubles at the 1998 U.S. Open.

Early in the 1999 season, Venus and Serena took the tennis world by storm. Serena won her first singles title at the Paris Open, and Venus won the IGA Classic on the same day! They became the first sisters ever to win tournaments on the same day. Then, two weeks later, Serena won her second tournament in a row, the Evert Cup.

On March 28, Venus and Serena met in the championship match of the Lipton Championships. It was the first time they had played each other for a tournament title. In fact, it was the first time that any sisters have faced each other for a title in 115 years. It was a tough, hard-fought match, with each sister winning one of the first two sets. Then, Venus won the final set 6-4 to win the championship. But Serena wasn't sad. She said, "I definitely look forward to another final with Venus. It's what we always dreamed of."

Serena (left) and Venus (right) leave the practice court at the Australian Open on January 21, 1998.

TIMELINE

VENUS

June 17, 1980	Venus Williams is born in Lynwood, California.
January 31, 1998	Venus wins the Australian Open in mixed doubles.
March 1, 1998	Venus wins the IGA Tennis Classic in doubles with Serena.
March 28, 1998	Venus wins the Lipton Championships in singles.
June 6, 1998	Venus wins the French Open in mixed doubles.
October 4, 1998	Venus wins the Grand Slam Cup in singles.
October 17, 1998	Venus wins the European Championships in doubles.
February 28, 1999	Venus wins the IGA Tennis Classic in singles.
March 28, 1999	Venus defeats Serena in the title match of the Lipton Championships.

SERENA

Sept 26, 1981	Serena Williams is born in Saginaw, Michigan.
March 1, 1998	Serena wins the IGA Tennis Classic in doubles with Venus.
July 5, 1998	Serena wins Wimbledon in mixed doubles.
September 10, 1998	Serena wins the U.S. Open in mixed doubles.
October 17, 1998	Serena wins the European Championships in doubles.
1998	Serena wins the WTA TOUR Most Impressive Newcomer award.
February 28, 1999	Serena wins the Paris Open in singles.
March 13, 1999	Serena wins the Evert Cup in singles.

 Serena (left) and Venus (right) hold up their trophies after the Lipton Championships on March 28, 1999.

GLOSSARY

African-American (AF–rih–kan uh–MAYR–ih–kan)
An African American is a black American whose ancestors came from Africa. Venus and Serena are African-Americans.

ghetto (GEH–toh)
A ghetto is a section of a city with similar people. The Williams family lived in a ghetto in Compton, California.

graffiti (gruh–FEE–tee)
Graffiti is words or pictures painted on walls. In the 1980s, Los Angeles had lots of spray-painted graffiti.

mixed doubles (MIKST DUH–bullz)
Mixed doubles are when a woman and a man play on the same tennis team together. Venus and Serena each have a mixed doubles partner.

ranked (RANKT)
When an athlete is ranked, he or she is given a number. The lower the number, the better the player is. Venus and Serena want to be ranked number 1 and number 2 in the world.

set (SET)
A set is a group of games. In women's tennis, the first player to win two sets wins the match.

sweep (SWEEP)
A sweep is winning all the tournaments in a group. Venus and Serena won all four Grand Slam tournaments, giving them a sweep.

unseeded (un–SEE–ded)
A seed is a rank for the top players in a tournament. When Venus and Serena were starting out they were unseeded because they weren't expected to win.

INDEX